PUFFIN BOOKS

THE TALE OF GREYFRIARS BOBBY

The Tale of Greyfriars Bobby is a strange and touching real-life story about a small dog and his master.

The old shepherd is more than a little disgruntled at first to have Bobby yapping at his heels. But the little Skye terrier is determined that this is where he belongs, and he will not let Auld Jock out of his sight. Whether Jock is minding the sheep on the Pentland hills surrounding the farm, or off on one of his jaunts to Edinburgh, Bobby is always close by – and there's nothing the poor man can do about it!

In fact, so dearly does the dog love his master that when the old man dies, his faithful friend watches over his grave in Greyfriars churchyard – every single day for fourteen years.

This enchanting retelling of the famous true story of *Greyfriars Bobby* has been especially written for Puffin to reach a new audience of young readers.

D1636310

LAVINIA DERWENT

The Tale
of Greyfriars Bobby

Illustrated by Martin J. Cottam

PUFFIN BOOKS

PUFFIN BOOKS

Published by the Penguin Group
Penguin Books Ltd, 27 Wrights Lane, London W8 5TZ, England
Viking Penguin, a division of Penguin Books USA Inc.
375 Hudson Street, New York, New York 10014, USA
Penguin Books Australia Ltd, Ringwood, Victoria, Australia
Penguin Books Canada Ltd, 2801 John Street, Markham, Ontario, Canada L3R 1B4
Penguin Books (NZ) Ltd, 182–190 Wairau Road, Auckland 10, New Zealand

Penguin Books Ltd, Registered Offices: Harmondsworth, Middlesex, England

First published 1985
10

Copyright © Lavinia Derwent, 1985
Illustrations copyright © Martin J. Cottam, 1985
All rights reserved

Printed in England by Clays Ltd, St Ives plc
Typeset in Linotron 202 Plantin

Contents

Chapter 1 Bobby Finds a Home 7

Chapter 2 The Big City 20

Chapter 3 The Tenement Children 36

Chapter 4 Greyfriars 50

Chapter 5 The Snow Dog 64

Chapter 1

Bobby Finds a Home

A carriage rattled along the twisty road towards the farm. Inside was a scruffy little dog, a Skye terrier who had seen nothing of the world and who had no proper home. The

people in the carriage wanted rid of him. They stopped outside the farmhouse.

'Is there a chance you might find a use for a wee dog?'

'No!' said the farmer. 'Not a silly wee dog like that!'

But no sooner had these words been spoken than the dog jumped down from the carriage and ran into the house. And into Elsie's heart!

Her father knew he was beaten.

'I give in,' he groaned.

Elsie sat at his feet, looking up at him with blue tear-stained eyes. As soon as he gave in, the sun came out and the tears changed to smiles. She had won!

Elsie was too young to make up long speeches, but she showed her pleasure by clapping her hands. 'The wee dog! The wee dog!' she repeated. 'I can keep the wee dog!'

Her father nodded. 'He's a daft-like beast,' he grumbled. 'If he had been a collie, now, he could have helped to round up the sheep.

But a terrier! What use will he be on a farm?'

Still, if his little daughter was pleased, that was the main thing. He smiled at her as she sat on the floor petting the small Skye terrier who was frisking round her. 'Good wee dog! Good wee dog!' she kept saying.

The dog licked her hand and wagged his tail. Then he darted away and sniffed into all the corners of the kitchen. It was a nice enough place and the girl was friendly, but he did not want to be a lapdog confined to the kitchen. He wanted more freedom. Freedom to go outside.

The farmer had gone out, leaving the door open. The little terrier scented the fresh air and the country smells. A hop-skip-and-jump! And he had bolted into the outside world.

'Wee dog! Wee dog! Come back!' cried Elsie, getting to her feet and toddling after him. But the wee dog did not heed her. There were too many new sights to take up his attention.

The immediate world was a farm on the Pentland Hills in Scotland, not far from the big city of Edinburgh. But the Skye terrier knew nothing of that. All he could see were sheep and some big dogs guarding them. That was enough for him! He had found something to chase. What could be better?

Yapping with delight, he darted towards the startled sheep and snapped at their heels. Bleating with terror, they turned tail and began to move out of his way. They could not understand what had gone wrong. They had been rounded up by the collies as usual, and were awaiting the next move from the shepherd who was in control of them.

There he was, standing as he always did, leaning on his big stick: his crook. When he saw the little dog he straightened himself up and let out an angry shout. Then he put his fingers in his mouth and gave a piercing whistle. The collie dogs understood his command and went bounding after the terrier.

They snapped at the little dog, and the terrier snapped back. It was all part of a game, the terrier thought. It was fun! He was enjoying himself when suddenly he felt something grip his throat. The shepherd had caught him by the neck with his crook.

The little terrier stared up at the man in surprise – an old man with a bent back and a

weatherbeaten face. He was shouting in a
gruff voice. Short sharp words.

'Away hame! Daft dog! Go on! Away
hame!'

'Hame' meant home. The terrier had found
a home all right, but that was only a *place*: a
warm kitchen and a lassie who wanted to pet
and pat him. All very well for soft silly crea-
tures like kittens or poodles; but *he* was a
Skye terrier and he wanted something better.
To be part of the real world outside. The man

with the long stick was more to his liking than the soft-spoken little girl.

No! he was not going back. He shook himself free from the shepherd's crook, and then he sat on his tail for a while watching the collies round up the straying sheep into tidy groups. The shepherd gave another whistle and they all moved off towards the hills.

'Wait for me! I'm coming too!' The little terrier went darting after them.

The old shepherd strode on, steadying himself now and again with his crook. He was used to long walks. Had he not trudged dozens of miles across rough ground in his day? But surely the hills were becoming steeper now . . . the stone walls round the fields – the dykes – were more difficult to climb, and his breath seemed to be shorter. The truth was, he was growing old.

His real name was John Gray, but the Scots called him Jock. He had once been Young Jock – but oh! that was many years ago. Then, he could run and wrestle and jump

with the best. The hills were not steep or the dykes hard to climb. He was the best shepherd in the district, trusted with the care and training of collie dogs. Think of all the prizes he had won at the sheepdog trials! One whistle, and the collies obeyed his commands.

Little wonder his master used to say, 'He's worth his weight in gold, Jock! The best shepherd I've ever had.'

But now they called him Auld Jock. 'Auld'

meant old; and there was no doubt he would never be Young Jock again. 'Aye! I'm getting auld,' he had to agree, though he tried to ignore it. It had been a good life, and he wished it would go on for ever. As long as he was out in the open air, with a dog at his heels, he was happy. And he still enjoyed a jaunt to Edinburgh, where he could have a drink at his favourite inn. There, he could forget his worries and escape from his sad thoughts.

But the time was coming when he would be forced to give up his work. He had overheard the farmer grumbling: 'Auld Jock's getting too old and slow for the job.'

Auld Jock knew he was being kept on out of kindness, but it could not last much longer. More and more he came to depend on the collies, until they did most of the work for him. He would whistle his orders, then rest on his crook till they ran the weary miles he was too tired to trudge.

Today he straightened his back and tried to put a spring in his step as he set off towards the higher slopes. He was clambering over a dyke when he heard a yapping behind him.

'That daft dog!' he groaned. 'Away hame! D'ye hear me? Away hame!'

The little terrier bounced up and down on his hind legs, pleased to be spoken to even in such a stern voice. Auld Jock kicked out angrily at him but still the dog did not flinch. He was not going to let the shepherd out of his sight.

As the old man climbed over the dyke, the terrier determined to scramble after him. It was not easy for such a little dog to jump so high. Try, try, try again! He fell back time after time; but at last with a triumphant yelp he reached the top. Down he jumped on the other side, and off he ran after the shepherd.

Auld Jock let out another angry shout and hit the terrier with his crook. The little dog took no notice and continued to follow at his heels. There was no going back for him now! He had found a master and would follow him for ever.

The old shepherd gave a grunt. 'Och weel! come on then,' said he, shrugging his shoulders. 'Ye're a daft beast, but if I canna get rid o' ye, keep ahint. D'ye hear me? Ahint!'

The Skye terrier soon learned that 'ahint' meant behind. So he stayed at the man's heels, stopping when the shepherd stopped and crawling forward when his master took another step.

But it was too tempting when a rabbit bobbed up out of a hole. The well-trained collies took no notice and did not move, but the terrier yelped excitedly and set off after his prey.

'Come back, ye daft dog!' roared the shepherd. 'Ye'll scatter the sheep. Ye canna gang bobbin' aboot like that. Keep ahint!' Then, as he moved off, he turned and said, 'Hoots! ye'd better have a name. Ye're aye bobbin', so what aboot Bobby?'

Now the shaggy little dog had a home and a name and a master to follow. He was not just a Skye terrier. He was Bobby.

And so began one of the strangest real-life stories about a little dog and his master.

Chapter 2

The Big City

Elsie was sitting on a rug in front of the kitchen fire. But where was the wee dog?

Outside, of course, following Auld Jock and the sheep.

He was always outside. Elsie had given up trying to keep Bobby in the kitchen. The terrier had tasted freedom and refused to be housebound. No amount of coaxing would lure him to the fireside. So she had to be content with her rag doll. 'But I'd rather have Bobby,' she sighed.

Suddenly she heard him barking outside, and a loud din at the door. It was the shepherd rap-rap-rapping with the handle of his crook. Then the door burst open and he pushed the terrier inside.

'Keep him in there!' cried Auld Jock crossly. 'Dinna let him oot! I'm on ma way to

the toon, and I dinna want that dog following me. Lock him in!'

He shut the door with a bang and was gone, leaving Bobby yelping and scratching to get out.

'Good wee dog!' coaxed Elsie, throwing aside her rag doll. 'Come and sit on the rug. Come on, Bobby. Good wee dog!'

But there was nothing good about Bobby. He was in a very bad temper. Why had Auld Jock left him? There was only one thing he wanted to do: to get out and follow his master wherever he went.

The shepherd was his best friend. For weeks now Bobby had run at his heels, happy to be out in the fresh air, living the active life that suited him. He was an alert little dog, quick to learn that every word and every whistle had a meaning. But there was no meaning if the shepherd had deserted him. Without Auld Jock he was lost.

Not that Auld Jock was soft with him. Bobby got more cuffs than kindness from the shepherd, as well as thumps from that fearsome crook. But he would sooner hear an angry shout from Jock than a gentle word from Elsie.

He was Auld Jock's dog, and that was it!

All this activity was making the little terrier strong and sturdy. He was finding it easier to leap over the stone dykes and to run the long miles without tiring. And he was trying hard not to rush after rabbits, but to stand still until Auld Jock gave the signal to move. Sometimes the other dogs turned and snarled at him, so he tried to keep out of their way in case he was tempted to bite back.

If he could please his master, that was all Bobby wanted. Now the old man had gone off without him! He must get out! If the door would not yield, he must try the window.

'Yap-yap-yap!' he barked in a frenzy, jumping up on to the kitchen table, then on to the window-ledge. 'Yap-yap-yap! Yap-yap . . .'

Meanwhile the old shepherd was striding

out on his way to Edinburgh. It was wonderful to get away on his own, without a daft dog yelping at his heels. Auld Jock looked forward to his visits to the big town, a change from the lonely life he led on the farm. He could mingle with the crowd gathered in the Grassmarket, he could watch them buying and selling, then wander off to the inn. Traill's Dining-Rooms. There he could sit at leisure, smoking his pipe and drinking ale before eating his simple meal.

Auld Jock whistled as he thought of it, but not the way he whistled to the dogs. This was a turn, 'Over the Sea to Skye'. The music kept him going. There were still many miles to walk, but it was not as tiring as tramping over the rough hillside. Soon he would see the spires of Edinburgh in the distance. He was getting nearer to his drink in the inn. 'Speed bonnie boat . . .'

Suddenly he stopped whistling. He had heard a sound behind him, a sound he tried to ignore. *Yap-yap-yap*! No! he would not turn round and look. Could it be Bobby? Surely the terrier could never have escaped from the kitchen, nor could he have run so many miles over strange territory. It couldn't be Bobby!

'Yap-yap-yap!' By now the dog was at his heels, barking with excitement. Auld Jock was forced to turn round. There he was!

'Daft dog!' he shouted angrily. 'Away hame! How on earth did ye get oot? And how on earth did ye find your way? Daft dog!'

Bobby leapt up and licked his hand. He had found his master, that was all that mattered. He had forgotten all his struggles to get out, his attempts to squeeze through the narrow gap left open at the window, his frantic barks and scratches. In the end Elsie had been forced to open the door and set him free. As for finding his way, well! he could scent the old shepherd for miles.

'Away hame, daft dog!'

Yet even as he spoke, Auld Jock knew he was wasting his breath. By now Bobby was running on ahead of him, looking back as if to say, 'Hurry up, Jock!'

The Skye terrier was so happy he could have danced all the way to Edinburgh . . . or wherever his master was going.

'You're a nuisance!' grumbled Auld Jock crossly. 'A perfect pest!'

But now that the terrier was here, what else could he do but continue on his way with Bobby frisking round him? As the road grew busier the old man called him to heel. 'Keep ahint!' he warned the dog gruffly.

Obediently, Bobby walked behind the shepherd, puzzled by the noise and bustle. Where had all these people come from? It was

a great change from the peaceful hillside. When they reached the Grassmarket the medley of noise grew louder. Crowds were milling about, dogs barking, children shouting, music playing. On the farm the loudest noise was a bird whistling or Auld Jock's sharp orders.

The shepherd marched on and went to join a group of men gathered near the market-cross. Bobby kept a wary eye on him, for he did not want to lose touch with him again. But there were many strange sights to divert the dog's attention.

The strangest was the hurdy-gurdy man, making music by turning a handle. *Tum-tum-tum*! It was a merry tune, and the children clustering round him began to jig up and down as if they were dancing. *Tum-tum-tum*! A little creature sat on top of the hurdy-gurdy. A funny wee animal, like a wizened old man, with a red tammy on his head. He was clapping his small paws and swaying in time to the music. *Tum-tum-tum*!

What kind of beast was that?

Bobby sat on his tail and watched in amazement. Then he heard an excited voice crying out: 'See the wee monkey! Oh! see the wee monkey!'

A lame boy squatting on the ground near by began to clap his hands in time to the music. *Tum-tum-tum*!

'See the wee monkey!' he chuckled, and turned to the terrier as if expecting some response. Bobby swished his tail. So the little creature was a monkey!

Geordie, the lame boy, was bouncing up and down, trying to dance like the rest of the children. For a time he had forgotten his pain and poverty, that he lived in the slums – called the Tenements – and seldom had enough to eat. The other youngsters pushed him aside when they were playing their rough games.

'Lame Geordie!' they sneered. 'We don't want *you*! You're too slow!'

Sometimes he thought it would be wonderful to be supple and straight so that he could run races and kick footballs. But at least he had fun looking on, and in the Grassmarket there was plenty to see.

The hurdy-gurdy man had moved away, so Geordie gave his full attention to the dog.

'Hullo, you!' he said in a friendly voice, dragging himself closer to Bobby. 'Are ye lost?'

No! Bobby wasn't lost, only bewildered by

the constant clamour. Suddenly he almost jumped out of his skin, startled by a loud booming noise. What was that?

Lame Geordie took little notice of it. He heard the one o'clock gun every day. The great cannon, Mons Meg, fired the shot regularly from the Castle ramparts. It was a signal everyone heard and understood.

Auld Jock heard it, too. Time for him to move off and make for Traill's Dining-Rooms to take his drink and dinner. Bobby cocked his ears when he saw his master walk away, and was off like a shot to join him. He was not going to be left behind.

'Oh! can ye not wait?' the lame boy called after him in a disappointed voice. He had hoped he had found a new friend who would share his loneliness; but Lame Geordie was used to his own company and was never downhearted for long. 'Maybe ye'll come back another day?'

Yes! Bobby would come back as often as his master came. Meantime he was dodging in and out of the passing people, always keeping the old man in sight. They passed a church called Greyfriars, walked through dark passages called 'wynds', turned right and left – and there they were. Traill's Dining-Rooms.

Mr John Traill stood at the door of the inn, enjoying a breath of fresh air and greeting some of the folk who came in. He was a man of few words, but he spoke briefly to his regular customers. He nodded to Auld Jock. 'Nice day!'

'Not bad!' agreed Jock, and went in to take his usual place on a wooden seat near the fire. It was a relief to sit down and rest his tired legs. He gave a contented sigh and put his hand in his pocket to search for his pipe.

The innkeeper stepped inside to attend to his customers, shutting the door behind him. Auld Jock was lighting his pipe when he heard a sound at the door. *Scratch-scratch-scratch! Yap-yap-yap!*

'What's that?' cried Mr Traill angrily. 'No dogs allowed in my inn! You know the rule!'

Auld Jock gave a weary groan. 'Aye, I ken!' he sighed and dragged himself to the door as the yelping and scratching grew louder. 'It'll be Bobby. I'll send him away.'

Send Bobby away! Auld Jock had scarcely opened the door before the little terrier darted inside, barking with delight at having found his master once again. No use trying to chase him out. 'I'm here and I'm staying!' was his attitude.

'Stubborn beast!' grunted the old shepherd. 'I'm sorry, Mr Traill. He'll no' budge!'

'I'll budge him!' roared the innkeeper, grabbing a broom. He began to chase Bobby in a fury of rage. 'Out! Out! No dogs allowed!'

No! Bobby would play games with the man if he liked, but he was not going out. He dodged between Mr Traill's legs, round the

counter, and then to a dark corner where he lay down with his nose on his paws. 'Nobody will budge me!'

In the end John Traill had to give up. 'I'm beaten!' he declared, throwing down the broom in disgust. 'That's not a normal dog. He'll have to stay this time, but he's never to come back again. Never!'

But despite the man's protestations, in the weeks that followed the little dog became as regular a visitor at Traill's Dining-Rooms as his master!

Chapter 3

The Tenement Children

'No, no! We dinna want you, Geordie. Ye're just a nuisance! Away ye go!'

The slum children who lived in a broken-down tenement pushed Geordie aside so roughly that the lame boy tumbled to the ground. He bit his lip and looked wistful for a moment as he tried to drag himself to his feet. But Geordie had heard it all before and knew it was true. He *was* too weak to join in the others' wild games.

In his imagination he could run faster than any of them. He could beat Big Tam at boxing, he could kick a ball better than Bob, he could turn cartwheels faster than Wee Eck. If only it was true!

In reality, he was forced to keep out of their way or stand at the back ready to catch a ball if it came near him. He was happy to pitch it back or try a feeble kick at an old tin can. Kick-the-can was one of their favourite games, played with an old cocoa-tin. Rounders was another, when they could find a rubber ball; and, of course, there was always fighting. The tenement children were seldom without bruises on their brows or cuts on their knees. It was all part of life in the slums. There was little else for them.

Except for Geordie. He was luckier than the rest because of his imagination. Better than that, he had a sense of humour. It helped him to forget his hard life, seeing the comical side of everything. Surely it was better to laugh than cry; and Geordie could always find something to amuse him, even though the others rejected him.

So today he pulled himself to his feet and looked around for something to entertain him. Suddenly he thought of the Grassmarket. That was the place to find amusement! Geordie cheered up when he remembered this was market-day. There would be crowds of people to watch, pedlars and performers, singing and dancing – and perhaps he would see the wee dog.

Over the past weeks, he and Bobby had often sat side by side watching the throng. The dog scarcely moved a muscle till he heard the one o'clock gun. Then he pricked his ears and was off like a shot, following the old shepherd, always in the same direction. To Mr Traill's Dining-Rooms.

Today it took the lame boy a long time to reach the Grassmarket, jostled by the crowds and sometimes knocked to the ground. He was bruised all over by the time he reached his usual place and saw that the dog was sitting there. Geordie gave a sigh of relief as he settled down beside Bobby. Yes! it had been worth all the effort to come. He could sit here for hours, just looking on and enjoying the sights. But first he greeted the little dog.

'Hullo, Bobby!'

The Skye terrier did not respond. He was too busy watching the crowds as if searching

for a familiar figure. There was such a forlorn
look about him that it touched the lame boy's
heart. 'What's wrong, Bobby? Cheer up!
You'll soon hear the one o'clock gun.'

That was what the dog would be waiting
for. The signal to rush off and join his master.
But why was the wee dog looking so sad?

BOOM!

The sudden noise was startling even
though it was expected. Children screamed,
the jugglers fumbled, pigeons flew dizzily up
into the air, and Bobby scampered off as if *he*
had been shot from the gun.

Lame Geordie watched him weave in and out of the crowd. There was something different about him today. *Yap-yap-yap!* He was barking in distress. Back and forward the little dog rushed, sniffing the ground and whining pitifully. What was wrong? Could he not find the old man?

'Dinna worry, Bobby; he'll turn up,' Geordie called to him.

The dog did not listen. He made one more search and then darted off in the direction of Traill's Dining-Rooms.

The lame boy sat and puzzled over it for a time. Something was wrong, but he could not solve the mystery. Where was the old shepherd? Then he cheered himself up with the thought that perhaps Bobby and his master would be reunited at the inn.

John Traill was standing in his usual place at the door of the inn, idly watching the passers-by. He greeted some of his customers as they came in. 'Hi, Tam!' 'Hullo, Pete!' Then he shrugged his shoulders impatiently when he heard Bobby barking in a frenzy.

'That dog!' he grunted angrily. 'He's a perfect pest!'

Bobby came bounding to the door, pushed past Mr Traill, and ran barking into the inn. First he rushed to the corner where Auld Jock usually sat, but the wooden chair was empty. The dog's tail drooped. He gave a whine and ran back to the innkeeper, pawing at his legs as if asking a question.

'No! I haven't seen him.' Mr Traill shook his head. Then he took a closer look at Bobby and cried: 'Mercy me! You're awful thin! Are you starving, poor beast? Wait! I'll get you something to eat.'

The food in the inn was simple, but there was an appetizing smell of smoked herring, roasted potatoes and stewed meat. The Skye terrier did not seem to notice it, but he waited long enough to lap up some water from a bowl. Then once more he ran off, whimpering as he went.

'Mercy me!' muttered John Traill. 'That

Bobby's a queer beast! I hope to goodness he finds the old man.'

It would not be for want of trying. The little dog did not confine his search to the Grassmarket; he ran all over the town, crossing unfamiliar streets, dodging in and out of the traffic, and causing a policeman to blow a blast on his whistle. Then Bobby squealed, like a baby crying, and ran back to the spot where Auld Jock often stood. His tail drooped when there was still no sign of his old friend. Where else could he search?

Then suddenly his ears were cocked, his tail was wagging, and all his weariness had gone. He had seen what he was looking for! An old man stumbled on unsteady feet across the cobbled street and turned in at a poor lodging-house. With a yelp and a bound, the Skye terrier set off after him. All his troubles were over; he had found his master.

But what was Auld Jock doing in such a wretched place? The inevitable had happened. The farmer had told the shepherd he

was too old and it was time to go. A young and
able-bodied shepherd had already been hired
to replace him. Auld Jock had been expecting
the blow, yet when it came it had almost felled
him to the ground. He had had to lean on his
crook for support as he faced the farmer.

What was he going to do? He had no friends or relations in the world; no one cared whether he lived or died. The only place he could go to was the big town of Edinburgh.

And he would have to go alone. He did not want that yapping little terrier following him. He wanted to be free of his old life and free of that persistent pest of a dog.

So Auld Jock spoke to the farmer. 'Could ye keep Bobby shut up till I get away?'

'Yes! Dinna worry, Jock. I'll shut him in the coal-shed.' It was the most secure building on the farm, with a door which could be bolted and barred. 'I'll keep him there for a couple o' days. Dinna worry! He'll no' get oot.'

Auld Jock set off alone on his last journey to Edinburgh. He had a small bundle on his back containing all his worldly goods. *It* was light, but his heart was heavy and his step slow. He could not bear to turn and look at the hills where he had spent so many happy years.

For the first time in his life the old shepherd had tears in his eyes. There was no spring in his step, no whistle on his lips; only a dull ache in his heart. His feet were faltering when he reached the town and he shuffled into the first inn he could find. Drink would help him to forget his troubles.

By the time Auld Jock came out of the inn, his step was unsteady and he was swaying from side to side. He had begun to cough – the cold wind was catching at his throat. Added to that, there was a pain in his chest, and he was finding it difficult to breathe. What he needed was shelter, but he had no strength to look for it. So he slumped to the ground and sat there, coughing and shivering.

At last the bitter wind revived him and he pulled himself to his feet to begin his search. By now he had lost his small bundle, but he found some money in his pocket and showed it to an old woman who kept a lodging-house.

'Come in,' she croaked, and lit a candle to

show him up the creaky stairs. 'Ye're in a bad
way, mister. Will I get a doctor?'

No! Auld Jock would have no doctor. All
he wanted was a bed to rest on, and to be left
in peace. But there was little rest or peace for
him that night. He tossed and turned, and by

morning the pain in his chest was worse and his lips were parched. But ill though he was, he dragged himself up and went out to a nearby inn to spend the last of his coins on drink. It was as he was staggering back to the lodging-house that Bobby caught sight of him.

The dog followed the old shepherd as he lurched up the stairs and opened the door of a dingy room. There was no furniture in it, only a bed in the corner which creaked when Auld Jock flung himself down on it. He lay there tossing, turning and coughing.

Bobby crawled forward and sat watching him. Then he went nearer and licked the wrinkled old hand. Auld Jock was aware of the dog's presence and began to mumble. 'Bobby! Is that you, Bobby? Daft dog! Gang away hame . . . Cough-cough-cough . . .'

Of course the faithful terrier had no intention of leaving his post. But he was so exhausted that at times he put his head down on his paws and drifted into an uneasy sleep.

Then he woke with a start when he heard that rasping noise. *Cough-cough-cough!*

'Keep ahint, Bobby! Cough-cough-cough! Gang hame! I'm too auld . . . too auld . . . Gang hame . . .'

The old man moaned in his sleep. His mind was blurred, but sometimes he had a vision of straying sheep and of dogs running at his heels. He tried to whistle and call: 'Come in ahint!', but he was too weak.

Bobby listened to the old man's ramblings as he crouched by the bed. Suddenly he sat bolt upright. Auld Jock was no longer coughing or wheezing. Why was it so quiet? Was his master cured?

No. Poor Auld Jock was dead!

Chapter 4

Greyfriars

'Quick, Geordie! Look oot! Catch the ball!'

The tenement children were playing one of their rough-and-tumble games. As usual Lame Geordie had been pushed to the back, but he was keeping a watchful eye on the others. If he was lucky he might get a chance to join in.

This was it! Now! The moment he had been waiting for had come. He would be a hero. Catch the ball deftly, and toss it back swift and straight to Big Tam who was waiting for it.

'Idiot!'

Big Tam let out an angry shout as Geordie dropped the ball. Why had he turned away and let it slip through his fingers?

'It's Bobby!' cried the lame boy.

The little dog had spent days roaming

through the Edinburgh streets. At last he had
come across a familiar face. He darted up to
the boy and pawed at his legs. The terrier was
whining so sadly that Geordie gave up his
moment of glory to attend to the shivering
little creature. He bent down to pat the dog.
'What's wrong, Bobby? Oh! poor wee thing,
you're starving!'

Geordie felt in his pockets, though he knew
he would find nothing there for the dog to eat.

'Wait, Bobby! I'll get something. Some water . . .'

But it was neither food nor water Bobby wanted. He was running round Geordie in great distress, as if he were trying to say something. What was it? The lame boy was at his wits' end trying to understand him.

He had a sudden idea. 'Come on, Bobby! We'll go to Mr Traill and see if he can help.' He knew the dog often went to the inn with the old shepherd. Perhaps the innkeeper would know what was wrong.

It was a long walk for Geordie with his lame leg; long and slow. The little dog bounded in front of him, barking impatiently. 'Hurry up! Yap-yap-yap! You're dawdling like a snail. Get a move on! Yap-yap-yap!'

Geordie limped on as quickly as he could. 'If only I could run!' he was thinking to himself. 'Oh! I wish I had a new pair of legs.'

He had lost his breath by the time he came within sight of the inn. Bobby was already there, howling on the doorstep. The din had brought Mr Traill to the door.

'That dog again!' he cried angrily. 'What's up with him? He's been at the door a dozen times already. What is he looking for?'

'I dinna ken,' gasped Geordie. 'Maybe it's the auld man. Bobby seems lost without him. Can you not find him, Mr Traill?'

'The auld man! Ye mean Auld Jock?' Mr Traill shook his head. 'I've got more to do than run after dogs and auld men.' But he was not as heartless as he sounded, and when he saw how distressed Bobby was he changed his mind. 'Come to think of it, I haven't seen Auld Jock myself for a while. Something must have happened to him. Maybe I should go and see . . .'

So he shut the door and set off with Bobby rushing on ahead, while Lame Geordie sank down on the steps to rest his weary legs. The dog was bounding and barking, impatient for the innkeeper to walk faster. 'Hurry!' he seemed to be saying. 'I've got something to show you.'

What could it be?

Mr Traill grew more puzzled as Bobby led him round corners, through narrow wynds and at last to the gate of an old churchyard.

'Greyfriars kirkyaird! What's Bobby wanting here?' wondered the man.

The little dog had left him and was trying to leap over the wicket gate, but it was too high. Then he tried to scramble up over the railings round the churchyard, but time and again he fell back with a whimper. The wicket gate was bolted and padlocked, and there was a notice above it. NO DOGS ALLOWED.

'Ye canna get in there, Bobby,' Mr Traill called out as the dog made another attempt to force the gate open. 'This is no place for dogs. Come back!'

But Bobby kept on barking and jumping as if he had gone mad. He tugged at the gate and scratched the ground in desperation. It was obvious that he was determined to get inside somehow or other.

Then John Traill saw it! A newly-dug grave roughly covered over. Could that be the reason for Bobby's strange behaviour?

'D'ye ken whose grave that is?' he called to a man who had come out of a nearby house.

It was James Brown, the keeper of the churchyard. He carried a stick in his hand, and his face was red with rage. Without bothering to answer Mr Traill, he rushed forward and roared, 'Get that beast away! NO DOGS ALLOWED! Can ye no' read?'

'The dog canna read! Hold it, man!' cried the innkeeper. The man had raised his stick and was about to bring it down on Bobby's

back. 'Answer my question. Who was buried in that grave?'

'Oh! some auld man,' said the caretaker impatiently. 'A shepherd, I think. I dinna ken his name. Auld Jock, they said! Aye! that's it!'

'Poor auld man!' Mr Traill shook his head sadly, thinking of the many times Auld Jock had sat at his fireside. Then he turned his attention to Bobby, whining at his feet. 'This is his dog,' he told the keeper. 'He's looking for his master.'

'Weel, he'll no' find him alive,' said James Brown crossly. 'Ye'd better take him away. NO DOGS ALLOWED. I dinna want to see that beast again. Get rid o' him!'

It was easy to say, but not so easy to do! No coaxing, no threats, no beatings would make Bobby budge from the churchyard gate. In the end, Mr Traill had to fasten a string round the dog's neck and drag him, howling, through the streets. The innkeeper was exhausted by the time he got home, and his patience was at an end.

'Get in there!' he shouted, pushing Bobby into a dark cupboard and locking the door. 'Ye can bide there till I get rid o' ye. I've had enough of you and your capers!'

But after a while his heart softened and he fetched some food and water. The dog was moaning in the darkness, but Mr Traill left him alone and went about his business.

He was serving his customers when he had

a sudden idea. A carrier who had left his horse and cart at the door came in for a drink.

'D'ye ken a farm, Cauldbrae, away up in the Pentlands?' he asked the man.

'Cauldbrae!' The man nodded. 'Aye, I ken it fine. I'm on ma way there after I've had ma dram.'

'Good!' said the innkeeper. 'I wonder if you could do me a favour? Could you deliver something to the farmer?'

'Aye, I could. What is it?'

'A dog.'

'A dog? Weel! I hope he's a quiet beast.'

Quiet! Bobby was making enough noise to rouse the whole of Edinburgh. For such a small terrier, it was surprising how much din he could make: barking, yelping, whining, scratching at the cupboard door, clamouring to be let out.

'Jings! that's a terrible racket!' cried the carrier. 'I doot I'll never get *him* in ma cairt.'

'Yes, you will!' John Traill was determined to get rid of the dog once and for all. 'I've got a

big hamper. We can shut him in that and lift it into the cart.'

Easier said than done. Bobby bit and scratched, growled and howled; and it took the combined efforts of the two strong men to control him. But finally they did it.

'That's it!' cried John Traill thankfully, when at last Bobby had been trapped in the hamper. 'Ye'll deliver the dog to the farmer? By rights he belongs to his wee lassie.'

The carrier wiped his brow. 'Aye, I'll deliver him! And right glad I'll be to get rid of such a noisy beast.'

Mr Traill gave a sigh of relief as he turned and went back into his peaceful inn. 'Good riddance! I hope I'll never see *him* again. I wonder what'll happen when he gets to the farm?'

But what did it matter? He was sure that he had seen the last of Bobby and could put the Skye terrier out of his mind.

But once more Mr Traill was to be proved wrong!

When the carrier finally reached Cauldbrae Farm, far away in the lonely Pentland Hills, he was only half awake. Worn out after his tussle with the terrier, and after jogging so many miles in his cart, he could scarcely keep his eyes open. For most of the journey the little dog had kept up a constant whimpering from the hamper in the back of the cart. But now to the man's great relief the noise had died down. Bobby had fallen into a troubled sleep, exhausted after days of wandering through the city streets.

When the cart drew up at Cauldbrae the

carrier called out to the farmer. 'Hi, mister! I've brought something for ye.'

'For me! What have ye got?'

'A dog,' said the carrier, heaving the hamper out of his cart.

'I dinna want a dog!' grumped the farmer. But when he raised the lid, he called out: 'Mercy me! It's Bobby! Help me into the house with the hamper, man. Elsie'll be delighted to see the beast again.'

Indeed, his little daughter was beside herself with joy. 'The wee dog! The wee dog's come back!' She clapped her hands and skipped around the kitchen. 'Oh! I thought he was lost for ever. Good wee Bobby!'

The little dog scrambled out of the hamper, still dazed and half asleep. 'Good wee Bobby!' cried Elsie, throwing her arms round his neck. 'Come and sit on the rug.' And she began to cuddle him as if he was her rag doll.

But Bobby was now wide awake. He shook her off and scurried round the kitchen like a

wild beast. Then he ran to the door, barking and scratching to be let out.

The farmer grabbed him and bundled him back into the hamper. 'None o' that!' he said sternly. 'Bide there till ye've learned some sense.' He turned to Elsie. 'Better give him something to eat. He's skin and bone, poor soul. Keep still, ye daft dog!'

Bobby struggled to get free while Elsie tried to feed him as she would feed a pet lamb, but after a while he gave up and settled down in the hamper. All the while he was watching and listening, biding his time.

At last it came! When everything was quiet, the farmer went out, leaving the door ajar. Bobby saw his chance! With a sudden spring, he leapt out of the hamper. The next moment he had escaped through the door.

'Oh! the wee dog's away!' cried Elsie as he slipped through her fingers. 'Come back, Bobby! Oh dear! I wonder where he's gone?'

Mr John Traill was soon to find out.

Chapter 5

The Snow Dog

For once the tenement children were not fighting. They were too excited at what had happened. Their whole world was changed.

'It's like fairyland!' cried Geordie, clapping his hands.

So it was!

Fluffy flakes of snow, as big as feathers, had fallen from the sky and settled on the houses. They were no longer slums; they had been transformed into pure white palaces where princesses might live. Not a cracked chimney or a broken window in sight! Everything looked new and glittering, as if the Snow Queen had waved a magic wand.

But it was bitterly cold. Geordie blew on his fingers as he admired the scene. None of the children had warm enough clothing to keep out the chill air. The best thing was to be

active, so the lame boy followed the others as they moved off in the direction of Greyfriars.

Geordie walked slowly, still in a dream. The white world enchanted him, and he stopped to gaze round at all the snowy towers and turrets that had not been there yesterday. Oh, it was beautiful!

Bang!

A snowball hit him full in the face. Big Tam had found a good target. By the time Geordie had bent down to make a snowball of his own, the children were out of reach and were shrieking; 'Come on! Let's build a snowman!'

The wicket gate leading into Greyfriars churchyard was buried under a mound of snow. Big Tam scooped handfuls away and began to build the snowman. Geordie limped forward and tried to help, but the others pushed him back. 'Not you, slowcoach! Out of the way!'

It was only what Geordie expected. 'Never mind!' he consoled himself. 'I'll build a snowman of my own.'

Then his imagination took over and he had a better idea. He would build a little snow dog! Why not? It would be fun to do something different.

He became so absorbed as he worked that he forgot all about the cold. The dog was taking shape. It was beginning to look like a terrier. A Skye terrier.

'It's like Bobby!' he cried, standing back to admire his work.

And just then a terrible thing happened.

The snow dog tumbled to the ground, and

all Geordie's patient work collapsed in a heap. He was so angry that he put up his fists ready to fight Big Tam, or whoever had knocked it down.

'Yap-yap-yap!'

Geordie could not believe his ears. Was the snow dog barking? No! it was a real dog. It was Bobby himself.

'Oh Bobby!' cried Geordie, trying to pick him up. 'Poor wee dog! You're frozen!'

The little terrier wriggled away and tried to climb up over the snow to get into the church-yard. Big Tam saw him. Here was another target! He scooped up a handful of snow, but Geordie stopped him. 'No, Tam, no! You're not to hurt the wee dog. Help him! He wants to get into the kirkyaird.'

'Hold on!' Big Tam left his snowman and picked up the shivering little creature. 'There! if that's what ye want, over ye go!' He lifted the dog over the gate and set him down inside the churchyard.

'Yap-yap-yap!'

At last Bobby had got what he wanted. He wasted no time, but ran at once to the spot where the old shepherd had been buried. He scrabbled in the snow with his paws; then when he had cleared the grave he lay down on top of it. He was near his master at last.

'Did I hear a dog barking?'

An angry man came rushing over the snow with a stick in his hand. 'Where is he?' he roared, waving the stick in a fury. 'No dogs allowed! Come on: tell me! Where is he?'

James Brown, the caretaker, was in a furious temper – even crosser than normal, for he had been forced to leave his warm fireside. Someone was going to suffer! He caught hold of Lame Geordie and shook him in a rage. 'Speak up, boy! Where's the dog?'

Geordie bit his lip, but he did not speak. He was not going to give Bobby away. The other children, too, were silent. They hated the loud voice of authority, so they ignored James Brown and continued to build their snowman. They were on the dog's side.

'Aha! There he is!' The caretaker had spied Bobby lying on top of the grave. He grasped his stick more firmly and began to pull the wicket gate open. 'Oot! I'll soon get him oot!'

'Oh! let him bide,' pleaded Geordie. 'He's not doing any harm. It's Auld Jock's grave . . .'

'No dogs in the kirkyaird!' roared the keeper, pulling the gate open. Big Tam threw

a snowball at him as he stumped forward to pick up the terrier. But James Brown ignored it, gripped the howling dog and dragged him away from the grave.

Outside the churchyard he waved his stick in the air, ready to bring it down on Bobby's back. But another snowball found its target. *Bang!* Big Tam scored a direct hit.

James Brown spluttered with rage. 'Stop it, ye wee deevils!' he bellowed, wiping away the snow. 'I'll get the police to ye!' And he began to chase the children, stumbling over the snowman, while they shrieked with delight and made their escape. But not before Big Tam had flung another snowball.

'Wee deevils!' growled the caretaker, turning on Geordie who had been left behind with the dog cringing at his feet. 'If ye dinna get rid o' that beast I'll . . . I'll . . . skin ye alive . . .'

Geordie was doing his best to keep the dog quiet, but he knew he could not control Bobby for long. As soon as James Brown's back was turned, the terrier was leaping up at the wicket gate, yapping to be let in.

And so it started all over again.

It was a pattern that was to be repeated day after day. For this was only the beginning of a battle that raged for weeks, months, and years.

But in the end the little dog won.

Auld Jock died long long ago, in the year 1858; and the faithful terrier kept watch over his grave for fourteen years.

Fourteen years!

'That's Greyfriars Bobby!' The passers-by stopped to point out the dog sitting on the old man's grave. He had become a familiar sight to the people of Edinburgh, as well-known as the one o'clock gun.

Every day when the *Boom* sounded, Bobby sprang up and ran round the churchyard as if in search of his master. Then back he darted and settled down on the grave.

James Brown still kept the notice NO DOGS ALLOWED on the gate, but he had

been forced to admit defeat. And as time went by, he grew to admire the little dog and even brought him bones to gnaw.

Lame Geordie and the other tenement children kept a watchful eye on the terrier and saved crusts for him to eat. They were always ready to help him over the railings on the few occasions when he left the churchyard. There was only one place he ran to: Traill's Dining-Rooms. John Traill had adopted the little dog and always had some food ready if Bobby came scratching at the inn door.

But Bobby never lingered over his meal. He gulped it down as quickly as he could, then barked as if to say 'Thanks' before hurrying back to his real home, Greyfriars churchyard.

And so it went on year after year till at last the little terrier fell into his final sleep on his master's grave.

But Greyfriars Bobby is still there for all to see.

A statue has been built near the old kirkyard. And there he is, the little Skye terrier, sitting as alert as ever, watching and listening for the one o'clock gun.

When the wind whistles at night it seems as if Bobby is cocking his ears. Does he imagine it is Auld Jock who is whistling? Wait! is that an answering sound?

Yap-yap-yap!

Could that be Greyfriars Bobby barking?

THE CONKER AS HARD AS A DIAMOND

Chris Powling

Last conker season, Little Alpesh had lost every single game, but this year he's determined it will be different. This year he's going to win, and he won't stop until he's Conker Champion of the Universe! The trouble is, only a conker as hard as a diamond will make it possible – and where on earth is he going to find one?

PUGWASH AND THE MUTINY and PUGWASH AND THE FANCY-DRESS PARTY

John Ryan

Two hilarious stories starring that most amiable of pirates, Captain Pugwash. When he and his cabin boy Tom are cast ashore, things don't work out quite as the mutinous crew had planned, for the dastardly Cut-throat Jake and his bloodthirsty band make an unexpected entrance. And that same evil villain is out to spoil Pugwash's devious plan for a fancy-dress ball – which would have filled the treasure-chest with gleaming gold, silver and jewels!

TALES FROM ALLOTMENT LANE SCHOOL

Margaret Joy

Twelve delightful stories, bright, light and funny, about the children in Miss Mee's class at Allotment Lane school. Meet Ian, the avid collector; meet Mary and Gary, who have busy mornings taking messages; and meet the school caterpillars, who disappear and turn up again in surprising circumstances.

TALES FROM THE WIND IN THE WILLOWS

Kenneth Grahame

'Isn't it a bit dull at times?' Mole asked Ratty. 'Just you and the river, and no one else to pass a word with?'

Mole couldn't have been more wrong about life along the riverbank. There were all sorts of animals living in and by the river, and one in particular who was anything *but* dull – Mr Toad! A delightful new edition, enchantingly illustrated by Margaret Gordon, and especially abridged for younger readers to enjoy.

ELOISE

Kay Thompson

Eloise is six. She lives at the Plaza Hotel (where her mother knows The Owner) with her dog, her turtle and her English Nanny. If there's one thing Eloise never is, it's bored. She never has a spare moment because there's just so much to do. There's the Lobby to check out, Skipper-dee's ears to plait, waiters and switchboard operators to help, French lessons to ignore and, above all, other guests to investigate. Eloise is wildly funny, wickedly inventive and totally unpredictable.

CUP FINAL FOR CHARLIE

Joy Allen

Uncle Tom turns up with a spare ticket for the Cup Final at Wembley. But will Charlie be allowed to go? In the second story, Charlie is given a brand-new pair of shiny red boots, which turn out to be far more useful than anyone could have imagined.

DUCK BOY

Christobel Mattingley

The holiday at Mrs Perry's farm doesn't start very well for Adam. His older brother and sister don't want to spend any time with him; they say he's too young. At first he's bored and lonely, but then he discovers the creek and meets two old ducks who obviously need help. Every year their eggs are stolen by rats or foxes, so Adam strikes a bargain with them: he'll help guard their nest, if they'll let him learn to swim in their creek.

THREE CHEERS FOR RAGDOLLY ANNA

Jean Kenward

Being a very special kind of doll, Ragdolly Anna is trusted to do all sorts of things for the Little Dressmaker – but somehow nothing ever seems to go right. Her balcony garden turns into a jungle, a misguided stranger hands her into a lost property office, and she's nearly bought as a fairy for a Christmas tree!

RETURN TO OZ

Alistair Hedley

Dorothy knows that her friends and the Emerald City must be saved from the evil Nome King, the cruel Princess Mombi and the terrifying squealing Wheelers. So, with some strange companions, Tik-Tok, Jack Pumpkinhead and a talking hen, Billina, she sets off on a frightening, mysterious and exciting adventure!

HANK PRANK AND HOT HENRIETTA

Jules Older

Hank and his hot-tempered sister, Henrietta, are always getting themselves into trouble, but the doings of this terrible pair make for an entertaining series of adventures.

FIONA FINDS HER TONGUE

Diana Hendry

At home Fiona is a chatterbox, but whenever she goes out she just won't say a word. How she overcomes her shyness and 'finds her tongue' is told in this charming book.

SEE YOU AT THE MATCH

Margaret Joy

Six delightful stories about football. Whether spectator, player, winner or loser, these short stories are a must for all football fans.